WAR
OF THE
THUNDER
GODS

WORKS BY TY'RON W. C. ROBINSON II

<u>BOOKS/SHORT STORIES</u>

DARK TITAN UNIVERSE SAGA

MAIN SERIES

Dark Titan Knights
The Resistance Protocol
Tales of the Scattered
Tales of the Numinous
Day of Octagon
Crossbreed
Heaven's Called
The Oranos Imperative
Underworld

SPIN-OFFS

In A Glass of Dawn: The Casebook of Travis Vail
Maveth: Bloodsport
The Curse of The Mutant-Thing
Trail of Vengeance
War of The Thunder Gods

ONE-SHOTS

Maveth, The Death-Bringer Mystery of The Mutant-Thing Shade &
Switchblade
Retribution of Cain
The Mythologists
Ambush Bot
Kang-Zhu
Cheeseburger Man
Tessa Balthazar
Elite 5

COLLECTIONS

Dark Titan Omnibus: Volume 1
Dark Titan Omnibus: Volume 2
Dark Titan One-Shot Collection
Dark Titan One-Shot Collection II

THE HAUNTED CITY SAGA

The Legendary Warslinger: The Haunted City I
Battle of Astolat: A Haunted City Prequel (KOBO Exclusive)
Redemption of the Lost: The Haunted City II
Helper's Hand: A Haunted City One-Shot

SYMBOLUM VENATORES

Symbolum Venatores: The Gabriel Kane Collection
Hod: A Symbolum Venatores Book
Symbolum Venatores: War of The Two Kingdoms
Symbolum Venatores: Elrad's Chronicles

A  UNIVERSE SAGA SPINOFF

WAR
OF THE
THUNDER
GODS

TY'RON W. C. ROBINSON II

CONTENTS

NOLDAR'S TRICKERY

I

Eragard, the first of the fifteen-dimensional realms to the Millennium Gods, ruled over by their all-father, Eden. Theus, the Millennium God of Thunder and the Son of Eden is the Prince of Eragard and the military commander, leading the Eragardian armies into battle while preparing himself to one day become the King of Eragard when the appointed time comes.

Theus, leading Lady Soya, the Millennium Goddess of War and the Mighty Trio, combined of Aslan, the Millennium God of Nature, Ornod, the Millennium God of the Brave and Bold, and Vanor, the Millennium God of Warfare and Violence made their way toward one of Eragard's open fields, primarily used for warfare. They approach, already having the knowledge of a battle, currently taking place between the Light Elves and the Dark Elves. Both sides have been warned about having their war on the fields of Eragard countless times in their history. Theus, approaching the commanding generals of both armies to get their situation straight. Theus, looked onward, seeing the elves in battle. Clashing each other with clubs and war hammers. Theus flies over toward them.

The elves continued their battle and gaze upward, seeing Theus hovering above them as his silver helmet shines and his dark blue cape flows with the wind. Erianor, the general of the Dark Elves pushed the elves aside to get in the center near Theus.

"Theus, Son of Eden!" Erianor yelled. "Why have you come and have chosen to interfere in our war against the Light Elves?"

"Take your warfare onto another realm's land, dark elf." Theus said. "This is Eragardian soil you're spilling elvish blood upon. We do not take it lightly."

Erianor waved his hand in a negative gesture toward Theus, mocking him and his words.

"Go back to your castle, Prince of Eragard and leave this battle to us to finish."

Erianor walked away as Theus stared at him. Theus' eyes slowly glow a thunderous blue with small fragments of lightning sparked from them.

"You did not heed my words, dark elf. I said leave!" Theus declared as he charged up a thunderbolt in his hand. Throwing it at Erianor, hitting him in his back. The bolt knocked Erianor forwards, falling to the ground after flying through the air by the strength of Theus' thunderbolt.

"You dare to assault me! A dark elf! How dare you, Son of Eragard!" Erianor said with anger. "You have made a big mistake for yourself, boy!"

Erianor and the remaining dark elves vanished into thick black smoke. Leaving only the light elves and their general, Eriador. Theus came down and approached Eriador.

"Seems you have more of a brain than your twin brother."

"Appears to be the case, Son of Eden. I will take my remaining brethren and we will leave your field at once."

"I thank you for your honesty and respect, General of the Light Elves."

Eriador created a portal made of elvish crystals. He and the light elves entered, returning to their realm in a flash of light. Leaving the realm of Eragard. The portal closed and Theus turned away, seeing Lady Soya walking toward him.

"What is it now, my Lady Soya?"

"You know the dark elves will return and Emperor Voldor might come alongside them this time."

"Then let him and his army come. We will deal with them ourselves. Maybe that's what the dark elves need. Some Millennium Gods to settle their score once and for all."

Theus flies into the air, returning to the city of Eragard and its palace.

In the wilderness outskirts of Eragard stood an abandoned castle. Aged and broken down. Within the castle sat Noldar, the Millennium God of Guile with his enchantress, Illianna, known as the Millennium Goddess of

Sorcery. Noldar had remained quietly in the middle of the trodden down castle that once belonged to an ancient sorcerer. When Illianna walked by his side, gazing her eyes into the portal Noldar had been staring into. Moving her dark and wavy hair to the side behind her shoulder.

"What are you gazing at now, Noldar?"

"I am preparing to open the portal to release my army upon Eragard. Theus and his lackeys have already dealt with the elf war. Now they'll have to contend with the wrath of Jontheim's finest arsenal. Frost Giants."

"Will Aurgelmir be attending this little get together party?"

"Aurgelmir is the one who gave me the opportunity to control his army and lead them into Eragard. So that they may destroy all who live therein and take some spoils back to their realm with them."

"When are they coming through the portal?"

"Right after the moonlight hits the top of Eden's golden palace."

In the portal Noldar and Illianna are staring into, they saw the army of frost giants, wielding frozen axes, hammers, and swords. Prepared and ready for Noldar's portal to open.

During the sundown in Eragard, Theus, Lady Soya, and the Mighty Trio entered the throne room where Eden and his wife, Meredith, the Mother of Theus and Queen of Eragard are sitting. They welcomed them into the throne room. They bowed before the king and queen of Eragard. Both wore their traditional royal garbs, paying honor and respect to the ancient Eragardians of old.

"Theus, our son." Eden said. "What is the news of the elves? Have they taken heed to the warning and left our borders as commanded?"

"The light elves did according to what we asked. But, the dark elves put up a fight. In truth, it was their general, Erianor. I took the small matter into my own hand and knocked him on the ground. Needed to make a statement. He didn't take kindly to it and said that he would return again to do battle with us or the light elves."

"Erianor has always been the stubborn, hotheaded creature of magic. Unlike his brother, Eriador, who has always shown respect toward us and any entities in the fifteen realms. Make sure that the dark elves to not return. Even if their emperor comes along with them."

Eden suddenly stares into space. For a moment, they question what he is seeing and after a while, Eden gets his focus back onto Theus and the others.

"Father, what is it?"

"Frost Giants are on their way! Make ready for war!"

Eden slammed his spear into the ground, trembling the castle and the surrounding areas of Eragard, awakening the people and the Eragardian soldiers. They made ready and stood outside of the palace, waiting for Eden to appear. Theus walked alongside his father as did Soya and the Trio.

"Frost Giants? How could they come here without anyone's notice?"

"Vindhler seen them coming through a portal. A portal

made of dark magic and he sensed it toward me and gave me the warning. When you become King of Eragard, you will also have this power. As you have little of it now. You just don't know how to use it yet."

They moved outside the palace and could see the dozens of Eragardian soldiers, standing and prepared for battle. Eden turned to Theus, directing him to the soldiers.

"Take these soldiers and lead them into the battle with the frost giants. I know for certain that with you leading the way, they will be unstoppable."

"I will father."

Theus raised up his Warhammer, known as the mystical weapon called *Mithrandir*. He held it up above his head.

"For the Realm of Eragard!"

The soldiers yelled the battle cry with Theus before heading off toward the portal in the distance fields of Eragard. Eden and Meredith watched Theus and the army march from the palace walls, entering the open fields.

"They've got this under control, Meredith. No need to concern yourself of this matter."

Theus and the Eragardian soldiers entered the open fields. Finding nothing in sight, Soya walked over to Theus as the Trio look around the fields.

"Where are the frost giants?"

"They're on their way. Just have to keep our eyes open."

"Who would allow them into our realm?" Soya asked.

"Our enemies. One crosses my mind."

A low thump echoed through the air as one of the soldiers screamed after being attacked and slammed by a frost giant's battle club. The portal revealed itself, with the frost giants stomping out in mass. All yelling and holding up their frozen weapons of war. Theus turned toward them as does the soldiers.

"Let's clean this field."

He flew toward the frost giants, diving right through them with the hammer in front. Going straight through the frost giants, cutting off limbs and ramming through the abdomens of a few. Lady Soya fought the frost giants with her sword called the Stormslasher. The trio battled the front giants in their fashionable pairs of three. Aslan killed them with his battle sword, Ornod used his battle club, knocking off their heads as he encountered, and Vanor with his battle sword, slaughtering the frost giants, leaving only their limbs remaining on the ground, melting away without a hint of heat.

Theus hovered in the sky and stretched out his arms, conjuring a miniature thunderstorm above the battlefield. Only a little moonlight was able to shine upon the battlefield. The lightning intensified as Theus directed the lightning against the frost giants. Lightning struck down upon the frost giants, who roared in pain. Their bodies in an intense burning sensation.

"Now, you will understand why I am called the Millennium God of Thunder!" Theus declared. "Now, feel the power of the storm!"

Heavy rain poured down from the clouds as the lightning struck many of the frost giants. Most made the attempt to run away, but are captured and killed by the Eragardian soldiers. Soya and the Trio finished off the remaining giants with Theus throwing his hammer at the last one, knocking its head off its shoulders. The hammer returned to Theus as the storm ceased and the moonlight shined upon the melting corpses of the frost giants.

In the distance of the field stood Noldar and Illianna. Noldar, holding his Guilespear, yelled in anger as he witnessed the frost giants' defeat by Theus and the Eragardians. Illianna could only stare at the field, seeing the giants' bodies turning into liquid and melting away into the blood-coated field.

"There will be another time for battle, my lover." Illianna said. "Just be patient with this."

"How can I be patient when the first order of business has failed! Never mind. I will speak to Hadi about this and what is possible."

"You're going to Abaddon?"

"Yes. Where else can I speak with Millennium Goddess of Death?"

Noldar vanished into a portal, going straight for Abaddon. Illianna took one last look at the field, seeing nothing but liquid. She waved her hands and disappeared into a thick green mist. Nowhere to be seen.

Noldar entered Abaddon, the realm of the dead, who

are neither honored nor dishonored. He walked through the dark, heated caverns of Abaddon calmly. Aware of the souls that are trapped to endure Abaddon for eternity. He approached the throne room and saw Hadi sitting. He made his way toward her, her two Death-Hounds growled toward him. Standing his guard. Hadi saw Noldar, commanding the hounds to stay down as she stood before him. Her tall presence and beautiful features brought a chill down Noldar's spine.

"So, this is Noldar." Hadi said. "The Millennium God of Guile."

"Yes, it is I. I am here to receive an audience with you concerning a troubling matter of my own accord."

"What does this matter of yours have to do with I, Guile God?"

"I need some assistance with eliminating Theus."

"The Millennium God of Thunder. He's your problem?"

"Aye. I need great assistance with defeating him so that I can rule over the land of Eragard."

"For this cause of yours, I surely hope you don't intend of making a mockery of me."

"I surely do not."

"I'll help you this once." Hadi said, as she waves her hands toward Noldar. Releasing an aura that surrounds him and enters his body.

"What just happened?" Noldar asked, looking around his body, feeling the odd energy.

"When you return to the land of the living, contact Lordi and Arnos. They will be your assistance in defeating Theus and conquering Eragard."

"Oh. Thank you, my death goddess." Noldar said.

He proceeded to walk away, but Hadi stopped him. Turning back to face her, she continued to stare at him with her dark red eyes, covered with the shadow of death.

"Do your work wisely, Guile God. Because if you do not take heed to your own words, you will end up here with me for eternity."

"I will not disobey."

Noldar left Abaddon through a conjured portal. Hadi sat in her throne. The death-hounds growled as she petted them.

Back at Eragard, Theus traveled to the Asbru, the one-dimensional portal between the fifteen realms. The gatekeeper, Vindhler could hear Theus approaching from behind.

"What brings you here?"

"Just to check on the sources of any other portals popping up around the fields."

"No. No portals so far. But there are some strange occurrences taking place in Eldigard."

"Such as?"

"Gods and heroes of their own. Showing up from the sky before the realm of Man. They're worshipping them as their new gods."

"Should I go down there to check things out?"

"In a matter of time, you will. Just not right now."

Theus nodded. Taking in Vindhler's words closely.

"Well, thanks for your trust and watchfulness, Vindhler."

Theus left the Asbru as Vindhler continued to keep a lookout into the fifteen realms of Eragard.

II

Noldar returned to his trodden down castle, using the power Hadi had given him to communicate with Lordi and Arnos. He used his portal device to contact them. Letting the power soar through the castle. Illianna entered, seeing Noldar. She ran toward him curiously.

"You're back." Illianna said. "What happened in Abaddon with Hadi?"

"She is willing to aid us in our mission to eliminate Eragard. She gave me this source of power to contact Lordi and Arnos to aid us."

"Very well. After you speak with the two, when do you plan to strike Eragard?"

"Right after I speak with Lordi and Arnos. Immediately after."

Noldar grinned. "No more waiting this time."

A small festival was held at the Eragard Palace with the celebration of the defeat of the frost giants. The people drank and partied as Eden and Meredith discussed plans concerning the realm and what can be done to protect it.

"In time, we will achieve peace in all the fifteen realms." Eden declared.

Theus entered through the scene, walking to his father's throne room. He opened the door seeing Eden inside.

"Father, can I have a word with you?"

"Yes, my son. Of course."

Theus entered the room, facing his father and mother.

"What is it?" Eden said.

"We haven't traced down the source that allowed the frost giants into our realm. We're still looking."

"The enemy will come when he or she decides its necessary. If it is a traitor in our midst, kill them when they present themselves. If it's an outsider, lock them up in the dungeon for future interrogation and judgment."

"I will see to that, father."

The doors shut behind Theus as he left. Walking outside, Soya approached him. He smiled at her presence. Relieved and calm.

"What is it now?"

"We have to find the one responsible for allowing the frost giants here. I sense we know who it is but I can't direct a finger toward him."

"So, it's a "he" that brought the giants in?"

"Yeah. I believe he's closer to us than what we intend to know ourselves. He knows all of us because he's been with us."

Theus began to sense something in the air. It's a heavy feeling. One of great weight. Becoming weary from the sense. Soya noticed him stumbling, as he attempted to stay standing.

"What is it?"

Theus slowly returned to normal. Taking in a breath and wiping the sweat from his forehead.

"A breach has been opened. Lordi and Arnos have been released from their imprisonment."

"Should I get the Trio prepared?!"

"Yes!"

Theus flew back toward the palace. Entering, he returned to the throne room to Eden and Meredith. Opening the doors and standing before them once again.

"You felt it too didn't you?" Eden said. "The tense air entering your body."

"I did. Lordi and Arnos's prison has been breached. They've escaped."

An explosion appeared from the city entrance. At the entrance is Noldar, wearing his dark green and brown armor with his ram-horned helmet. Illianna stood beside him and behind them is Lordi and Arnos. All four prepped and battle-ready. Theus gazed toward the entrance from the palace, seeing them. Soya and the Trio also see them. Theus moved with haste as Soya and the Trio followed him.

"Noldar!"

"What do you need us to do, Theus?" Ornod asked.

"We head straight for them and finish this mess."

Theus flew up into the sky toward the entrance with Soya and the Trio following him from behind as Eden watches onward with Meredith at his side.

They left the palace, heading toward the city entrance. Meanwhile, Noldar, Illianna, Lordi, and Arnos entered the city of Eragard and began slaughtering the those around. Screaming in horror as they're being destroyed. Arnos sliced them with his battle axe as Lordi injected them with a drug, causing them to have deceptive hallucinations and making them believe he's come to protect them. They walked toward him in deception, he snapped their necks one by one.

"Tis' good to be back in the land of Eragard." Lordi gestured. "Wouldn't you agree, Arnos?"

"I do. We can do so much out here to make a statement to all the fifteen realms."

Noldar smiled as he witnessed the carnage unfolded. He turned to Illianna with a bright smile.

"This is the beginning of our salvation, my love! Eragard is ours!"

Thunder roared above them, gaining their focus. Noldar reluctantly glanced up in the air, seeing Theus, Lady Soya, and the Mighty Trio. Illianna looked upward and stared. As did Lordi and Arnos with anger in their eyes. Fire engulfed their insides.

"He's finally come." Noldar said. "The great Theus Edenson!"

"He brought his whore alongside him, my love." Illianna said, gesturing toward Soya. "I'll deal with her."

"Noldar!" Theus said. "I should've known you were behind all of the troubles we've been experiencing."

"Of course, Edenson! Who else could derive such a plan that would send you and your friends into utter chaos? Only I, Noldar, the Millennium God of Guile could do such a thing and all of you know it!"

"End this now, Noldar. Before the consequences before worse."

Noldar grinned. Loving how his plan is working.

"It will end, Theus. Just not the way you're expecting it to end."

Lordi and Arnos flew into the air to combat Theus. Arnos raised his axe, smashing it into Theus, knocking him down toward the ground. Soya flew toward Illianna and they engage in combat. Noldar stared at the Trio as they land on the ground in front of him. Three against one. Noldar loved those odds.

"Which of you will fall by my hand first?" Noldar said.

"I'll take the first hit!" Ornod said. "Get ready to fall, God of Guile!"

Ornod went for the swipe with his battle club toward Noldar, who made his body transparent, the club swung through his body. Noldar hardened himself together and raise his Guilespear, swiping it in the back of Ornod's head. Knocking him out. He faces the remaining two, Aslan and Vanor, smiling at them.

"Next?" Noldar asked with a big, sinister and happy grin.

On the other side of the city, Illianna and Soya fought, slamming each other into structures. Illianna flew toward Soya, yet, is struck with a right heel, knocking her into a wall.

"You always used your legs for everything." Illianna muttered. "Shame."

"And yet, you're the one who's lying on the ground." Soya said. "Stand up and face me like a woman, witch!"

"With pleasure, whore."

Illianna stood up, snatching Soya by her cape, punching her and threw her into a building. Illianna later controlled some of the nearby people, making them attack Soya. She fought them, but she refused to kill them before she was kicked in the back by Illianna.

Theus is double-teamed by Lordi and Arnos. Using their abilities to pummel him into the ground. They jeered as they proceeded to beat Theus into the ground, deepening him into the ground. A proper burial place.

"You thought we could be kept in a prison?!" Lordi gestured. "You fool!"

"We're Millennium Gods just like you!" Arnos said. "We have power beyond what many comprehend!"

"Yet. You have no trait of intellect nor instinct." Theus

said. "Allow me to show you what it truly means to be a Millennium God."

Theus charged up his power within his hands and shoved Lordi and Arnos from him. Through the flying dirt, Theus stood with Mithrandir in hand. He lunged toward Arnos, slamming him with Mithrandir into the ground. Making a quick right turn to swipe Lordi across the city. Theus hovered into the air and released crashing thunderbolts, striking Lordi and Arnos.

"Feel the power of the thunder!" Theus yelled as he released a stronger lightning bolt from Mithrandir, striking Lordi and Arnos.

Noldar began to face Aslan after defeating Vanor with an illusionary attack. While fighting Aslan, Noldar notices Lordi and Arnos have been defeated by Theus. Due to the lightning in the sky.

"No!" Noldar said. "Where's Illianna?! My love, where are you?!"

Upset, he searched for Illianna and saw Soya walking toward him. He can see she's dragging something with her. He looked closer, Soya is dragging an unconscious Illianna. Knowing his plan is failing, Noldar tried to run, but is cornered by a revived Ornod and Vanor. Surrounded by the Trio and Soya, the spark of thunder sounded from above him. He glared up as Theus came down from the sky.

"You got me this time, Edenson." Noldar said somberly.

"You're coming with us. For judgment."

Theus grabbed him, returning to the palace.

Within days, Noldar's judgment took place. Eden had placed Lordi and Arnos into a deeper state of imprisonment. To where neither Millennium God nor gods of any kind could break them out. Illianna had been thrown into a dungeon for a period of a year in the sight of the gods. Eden commanded Noldar be brought up before the Eragardian council.

"By the laws of Eragard, you, Noldar Thanatoson, Millennium God of Mischief and Guile, will be placed into the dungeons of Eragard until the necessary time for your release." Eden said.

The guards entered, snatching Noldar by his arms, pulling him out of the council's sight and to the dungeons. While walking down the alleyway of the dungeon, Noldar looked over at the cells, spotting those who are imprisoned, from trolls to demons to cyclopes to aliens and to Illianna herself.

"We will get out of here, my love." Noldar said. "I promise you!"

He made the attempt to approach her cell and the guards snatched him away from Illianna.

"Keep walking, Guile one."

The guards placed Noldar into his cell and shut the door. Locking it. They walked away as Noldar stared down the alleyway. He hung his head while standing in the middle of the cell. A split second after the guards left the dungeon corners, Noldar smiled.

"I'm inside." Noldar said. "Just as we agreed."

WAR OF THE THUNDER GODS

CHAPTER ONE: THE SHOWCASE OF POWERS

Within the starry skies of Eragardia, the fifteen realms seemed to be at peace. Peace however was not commonly seen amongst the living in these days as the ongoing war of the elves continued to be in flux across Elfheim, ream of the Light Elves and ruled by Emperor Aeden and Svartheim, realm of the Dark Elves, dominated by Emperor Voldor. The war had concluded with the elves seeking a truce to never step beyond the boundaries of their respective realms and into the others unless of a dire circumstance. One that may be of the end of all things.

Now, the Millennium God of Thunder, Theus had traveled across all the fifteen realms to keep them in balance as many sought to eliminate his power to invade Eragardia itself. Theus aided the Light Elves in their fight against the Dark Elves. After the Elves' War was complete, Theus entered Eldigard, known as Earth and met the risen heroes who dwell within. Joining them to form the unit called The Resistance, Theus continues to return to Earth and aid them in matters which deem more fit for a godly battle than a human's war. Helping the heroes take down his primary adversary, Noldar the Millennium God of Guile with Death, Kex Kendrick, King Stroh The Conqueror, Octagon, and the Blacholian force of Oranos. Theus bid the heroes farewell as he returned to his own realm.

A prepare for war was made after an unseemly warning erupted from the realm of Bidavellir as Ukko, one of the mighty trolls who dwells within the realm has sought out the challenge of facing the Eragardians in battle. His army was set and ready for the arrival of Theus and his comrades. Within days, Ukko waited. His patience growing thin as the moon and sun above him continued to set day by night with no sign of the Eragardians nor the spark of their coming power. Ukko began to grow tired. Walking out into the open lands and screaming into the air for the arrival of the Eragardians. He began to shout their names and curse them under the sun.

Yet, seven days later, a loud boom screeched thought eh clouds above Bidavellir, calling out Ukko from his home. His mighty war-hammer in hand as he gazed toward the sky and saw several streaks of light. Unsure as to what they could be, he knew they came from Eragard and he was proud as a grin formed on his large face. Rallying his army as they smashed their hammers against their shields, seeing the lights coming closer toward the ground. Ukko stood in front of the army, sealed in his burnt silver armored from his neck down. The lights inched closer, nearly bright enough for the army to cover their eyes. Ukko was not afraid as he let the light shine.

"Come Eragardians!" Ukko screamed. "This day, the

land of Bidavellir shall relish in the taste of your blood!"

The light brightened and crashed into the dirt, forming a crater before the sight of Ukko and his army of trolls. The air around them was shrouded in flying dirt and debris as it cleared, unveiling Theus, Lady Soya, and the Mighty Trio of Aslan, Ornod, and Vanor before the sights of the trolls and Ukko. Theus arose from his knees and faced Ukko with lightning sparking from his hands and eyes.

"The Millennium God of Thunder." Ukko spoke. "You've accepted my proposal."

"You curse our names toward the sky. Continued to beg for our arrival and for what cause? So, that you would be defeated by the hands of Eragardia's finest?"

"No! I will not fall this day! I, Ukko, Maser of Bidavellir summoned the might of Eragardia to prove you're no longer required to be the protectors of the realms."

"And you're seeking to place yourself above all others?" Lady Soya asked. "Without any forms of test? No trials?"

"I need no tests nor trials to prove my worth! The weapons I've formed are a perfect match for anyone who opposes me. You will learn how this day."

Theus reached toward his back and raised up his hammer simply known as Mithrandir. The hammer sparked with lightning as it surged from Theus' hands and to the head of the war-hammer. Ukko gripped his hammer and slammed it into the dirt.

"Ready when you are." Soya said to Theus with a smile.

Theus grinned, leaping up into the air and causing the thunder to crack as rain began to fall upon the field. Ukko grunted with a stomp as he commanded his army of trolls to attack Soya and the Trio. The four Eragardians savored the notion of the incoming army and ran into battle. Clashing their blades against eh shields of the trolls. Over on the other end, Theus crashed down several feet in front of Ukko as the mighty troll swung his hammer into Theus' own.

"No godly powers will defeat me."

"I've dealt with you once before, Ukko. His time will not be any different."

Theus shoved the weight of Ukko from his hammer and jumped into the air, crashing the hammer down upon Ukko's own as the shockwave of lightning spun out across the battlefield with streaks of lightning crashing down upon the grounds. On the other end, Lady Soya relished the moments of slaughtering the trolls with her blade. A delicate moment. The Trio did the same with each of their skill sets proving useful in the fight against a mass of trolls. No different than the dark elves in battle, only much larger.

"These things never learn!" Ornod screamed in battle.

Theus moved swiftly with the lightning which he expelled toward Ukko. Flowing through the mid-air, gilding in a sort. Ukko screeched as he hurled his hammer toward the Millennium God, only for the hammer to return to him in force. Smashing him against the wall of the mountain. With Ukko on the ground, Theus lowered himself as he approached the downed troll. Walking closer, the crack of thunder in the air alarmed everyone on the battlefield, even Theus himself.

"Was that you?" Soya asked Theus.

"No. It was not me."

The thunder cracked once more as two beams of light entered the atmosphere, heading towards the battlefield. The Trio moved from the path as did the army of trolls.

Ukko stood up and faced the beaming lights as did Theus.

"More of your forces?" Ukko questioned.

"Not mine." Theus replied. "Yours?"

"Hmph. No."

The lights had reached the ground and crashed, bringing up the dirt and the smoke around them. Blinding their sights. However, Theus raised up his opened hand and sparked a huge beam of lightning around the field, blowing away the dirt and smoke. With the scenery clear, what everyone saw standing in the midst of the field were two figures. Each one wielding a weapon of their own. The first was burly in size, holding a hammer of great strength. His beard and hair flowed with his gleaming armor. The second was leaner in stature, yet stern. Unlike Zhor, this one wasn't fully clad in armor. He wore the garments of a hunter. Skins and fur were his attire and they suited him well. Holding a axe/hammer hybrid in his right hand, holding it over his shoulder. Both their eyes were centered upon Theus and him only. Not even a turn or glance toward Ukko, Soya, the Trio, or the trolls.

"Who are they?" Aslan wondered.

Theus moved forward, facing them. His hammer set on his side.

"State your names."

The burly one took a step forward, placing his hammer on the ground to a sudden quake. His eyes locked with Theus.

"I am Zhor! The God of Thunder!"

Theus stepped back hearing the words which had come from this Zhor. A god of thunder? Soya went to press forward, yet was held back by the Trio in case of a coming battle. As they are aware of what happens when gods of the same stature collide in combat. A sight not even the humans have yet to witness.

"And what about you?" Theus asked the second one.

"I am Taraino. The God of Thunder."

Theus gave them a nod of confusion.

"I believe the both of you are mistaken. I am Theus, the Millennium God of Thunder. The powers of the heavens are mine to control. No one else's."

"You dare deny us our heritage?!" Zhor pressed himself. "We are thunder gods! It is why we are here!"

"Then, we shall take this matter of Eragardia. Let us see what my father Eden has to say concerning your heritages."

Zhor took a moment to pause himself and think. Taraino had already agreed to Theus' suggestion. Zhor stared and later gave a nod. Theus nodded back as he turned to Ukko and warned him to get control of his army and resist not causing another disturbance. Ukko agreed to the truce due to the interference of the foreign gods. From there, Theus and the two gods alongside Soya and the Trio left for Eragardia.

CHAPTER TWO: A HERETIC ENDEAVOR

Moving through the Asbru before touching the skies of their home-world, Theus made his return to Eragardia alongside the two mysterious thunderers. Making their way toward the palace where Eden himself awaited Theus' return. His eyes keen on the two other figures. Upon their landing at the palace steps, Eden hugged Theus and greeted Soya and the Trio. Once Eden arose from embracing his son, he stood firm and focused his gaze toward the two foreign gods.

"Who are these men?" Eden questioned. "I sense a strange power from them."

"Father, they came from the skies during our battle with Ukko. They claim to be thunder gods themselves."

"Thunder gods? From where?"

"I understand this may all seem a bit difficult for all of you to comprehend." Taraino spoke.

"I will not allow you to utter a word until we are inside." Eden commanded. "As long as you're out here amongst the ears of my people, I will not tolerate a foreigner speaking their ideals."

Taraino stepped back and nodded. Eden took the response as a show of respect. From there, he proceeded to allow the two gods into the palace to speak their peace regarding their sudden appearance. Soya and the Trio were commanded to head to the other ends of Eragardia to prepare for a possible war against a foreign entity that may be related to the two gods. Theus, on the other hand spoke to Eden he would like to have a word with Noldar, the Millennium God of Guile who's still imprisoned after his bout with The Resistance and the Protectors on Eldigard.

Walking inside the palace, the sheer glow of gold was everywhere. The two gods wondered where such gold had originated from. For they have never seen so much in one place. Eden sat on his throne with Meredith by his side. His spear in hand as the two thunder gods faced him. Eden sighed as he measured them. Their weaponry and their countenance.

"Your names." Eden said. "Tell me of them."

"I am Zhor."

"Zhor?!" Eden responded. "And you're a thunder god?"

"I've been called the *Estranged God of Thunder*."

"Estranged? By what kinds have spoken of you in such a manner?"

"Those who do not understand my plight."

Eden nodded while glancing down on the golden floor toward Zhor's blundering hammer.

"And what of its name?"

"The hammer?"

"Yes."

"I've come to simply call it, the *Mallet*."

"Mallet. Huh. And why have you given it such a boastful name?"

Eden took a small liking to Zhor, although not as much

as Zhor would perceive the King of Eragardia to give him. Eden turned his focus toward Taraino, who remained silent and still. His eyes and gaze centered upon Eden and not even a gaze nor turn toward Zhor. It was almost as if the two thunder gods appeared at the same time, were yet on opposite agendas and Eden knew this to be true.

"And your name?"

"My followers call me Taraino."

"Taraino." Eden nodded. "And you're a thunder god as well?"

"*The Primeval God of Thunder.*"

"Primeval?" Meredith paused.

"You're saying you've been around for eons. Ages of war you've fought?"

"I have."

Eden took another look at the two gods and nodded.

"Tell me, what brings the two of you here to Eragardia?"

"I was sent here for a great cause." Zhor spoke.

"A great cause?" Eden paused. "What kind of cause would send you to the dominion of Eragardia?"

"I was told there could be only one thunder god and I summoned enough power to transport myself to a place where the most dominate thunder god could be found."

"Ah. You speak of Theus. My son and the rightful thunder god."

"I've come to take him on in combat. Defeat him and claim the rightful title of God of Thunder."

"I see. You've come from a land I do not know to challenge a Millennium God for the right of his title?"

"Rightfully my title."

"I have to disagree." Taraino said. "I've been around

much longer than this Zhor. If anyone is worthy of challenging the Millennium God of Thunder, it shall be I."

Zhor turned toward Taraino with anger kindling in his eyes. His hand twitching for the grip of his hammer. Taraino stood calm. No emotion. No expression. Eden watched on as the two foreign gods stood opposite of one another. The energy surging from them both gave Eden a great understanding to their purpose.

Elsewhere in Eragardia, Theus arrived inside the prison and approached the door in which Noldar stood behind. Knocking for the door's opening, Noldar stood against the dark walls of the cell as the door creaked opened, allowing Theus to enter with two Eragardian guards standing by the sides of the door. Noldar looked at Theus entered and greeted him with applause. Not of truth, but of mockery.

"Tell me, what brings the Prodigious Theus to my cell?"

"It appears we have visitors."

"Visitors? Of what kind are you referring to? Celd? Death? Kendrick?"

"No. Two individuals who proclaimed themselves to be gods of thunder."

Noldar's eyes had widen to the sound of the words.

"You're telling me you're not the only one? Aside from Zeus that is."

"There's something off about them and every time something like this occurs, it always has your hand upon it."

"That is true for a number of things. Although, this

time it is not."

"That so?"

"I have no clue who these two thunder gods may be. Why would I consult in them when I already have a hard time dealing with you."

Theus grunted with annoyance in his breath to Noldar's own selfish amusement.

"You have nothing to do with this?"

"Nothing. I swear to Eden himself. I have nothing to do with these foreign gods you've met."

"Very well."

Theus went and took his leave. Stepping out of the hallway to make his exit, one of the guards approached him with haste. Theus recognized the motive from the guard as he's seen it in others before.

"Son of Eden, word is requested for you."

"Of what kind?"

"Emperor Voldor of Svartheim requests your presence in his realm."

"The Dark Elf seeks to have an audience with me?"

"Yes, my lord."

"Thank you for the message."

Theus went and returned to the palace to inform his father of the news. While reaching the palace, the guards standing at the entrance told Theus of Eden's current conversation with the two foreign gods. Seeing as he did not want to disturb the meeting, Theus went to the Asbru to make his preparation. Walking the Asbru center,

Vindhler stood by and acknowledged Theus' presence.

"I see you received the message."

"Yes, Vindhler. I need to get to Svartheim. Emperor Voldor wishes to speak with me. Not sure why."

"He knows of the foreign ones."

"He does? How?"

"That is a question you will have to ask him yourself."

The Asbru glowed and brightened with a rainbow-hued light. The trail was open as Theus stepped through the light and onto the Asbru, instantly transporting him to Svartheim.

Seeing the realm covered in shadows of darkness with the humming sound of the dark elves marching on the fields preparing themselves for a coming battle. Theus kept himself to the skies to get a look across the realm. Seeing the palace in the distance, glowing in the glistening darkness of violet and grey, Theus flew toward it and arrived to the confrontational surprising from the dark elf guards.

"I have not come to fight. Your master has requested my presence."

The guards lowered their spears and stepped aside as Theus entered the palace, sensing the presence of Voldor. Following one of the maidservants into the throne room, Theus looked on, seeing other dark elves clothed in wealthy garbs. He's never seen dark elves with such notion of fashion. The throne room doors opened for the maidservant to lead Theus in and once inside, Emperor

Voldor sat on the throne, glaring toward Theus.

"He has arrived, my lord."

"Thank you for bringing him in." Voldor replied. "Leave us. All of you."

The maidservant and the guards took their leave from the throne room as Theus stood center in the room while Voldor laid back in the chair. The doors closed to a gong. Theus kept his eyes on Voldor, seeing him dressed in his elvish armor. The gleaming light from above shined down upon him, brightening the armor's presence before him.

"You sent word for me." Theus said. "What do you have for me?"

"I know about those foreign gods who are currently within Eragardia. I sense a grave danger from them both."

"Do you? And do you happen to know where they came from or anything related to their arrival?"

"I only know they're not from our worlds. None of the fifteen realms."

"None? Such a thing is not possible."

"I'm here to tell you, it is possible and it is true."

Theus nodded, taking in Voldor's words.

"Then, is that the reason you summoned me here? To tell me these foreign gods originate from a place I do not know?"

"Yes."

"If that's the case, there exists an alternative. A way to return them from where they came."

"There is."

"I take it you know the way." Theus spoke.

"Combat."

"Combat?"

"These foreign gods came here for one reason and one

reason alone. To see who the definitive thunder god is. Between the two of them and yourself, a battle must take place. A winner must be chosen to end all of this."

"I do not understand any of this." Theus replied. "Zeus isn't here. If this was a battle between gods of thunder, he should've arrived as well. Not just these foreign gods and I."

"On that, I have nothing to add. Although, I am sure you have several allies from the Olympian realm. Perhaps, they can offer you some details to this growing war of the thunder gods."

Theus remained silent as his mind wandered. Within a few minutes, a thought entered his mind as he raised his eyes toward Voldor.

"I have someone in mind."

"Good of you to know. Now, I've told you all I know. Our conversation is complete. You may leave my palace and my realm now."

Theus took a pause. His right fist balled up as his hammer rested on his left side. Voldor stood up to the sound of his rattling armor.

"I do not wish to fight you, thunder god."

"Nor do I. Yet, you stand ready to battle."

"Only if you make a quick move of haste."

Theus grinned.

"Nothing from me. Thank you for the information, Voldor."

Theus exited the throne room as Voldor returned to the chair.

From there, Theus flew over the palace and saw most of Svartheim. Gazing up to the skies, Theus called out to

Vindhler as the Asbru returned to him, transporting him back to Eragardia.

"Was Voldor's information enough for you?"

"Enough to a point. Vindhler, I need to make a quick stop to Eldigard. to speak with someone who has some information concerning the Olympian pantheon."

"I know who you're heading out to speak with."

"He knows a thing or two about them. I'll be back."

Vindhler gave Theus a smirk as the Asbru sent him to Eldigard. The sky beamed with light to Theus' arrival.

The light emitting from the Asbru was nearly brighter than the sun during the noon of the day. Hovering in the air, Theus looked ahead and saw the glowing fortress. Flying toward it, he arrived in time to find someone entering the fortress. Landing on the ground, Theus walked into the fortress and saw all the weaponry which sat inside. He recognized several of the blades, knowing them to have come from the armory on Mount Olympus. Approaching the weapons for a closer gaze, Theus is stopped by the sound of a voice.

"I wasn't expecting you to have come here. Let alone find this place."

"Ah. Taltus the Titagod. Good to see you once again."

Taltus and Theus greeted one another with a hug. A Millennium God to a Titagod.

"Seems you're doing well after our battle with Oranos."

"Doing best as possible." Taltus replied. "So, what brings you to my fortress?"

"There has been an unsettling turn of events back on Eragardia. Two gods. They proclaim to be gods of thunder."

"Zeus?" Talus asked without question.

"No. These gods call themselves Zhor and Taraino."

"I've never heard of them before."

"I need to know if you're aware of any other thunder gods within the Olympian pantheon. Or imposters of a kind."

"I know only one thunder god from Olympus. Only one."

"I see. Well, I'm not sure where they come from. But, what I do know is they cannot remain in Eragardia any longer. They want a battle from what I've been told."

"And will you? Battle them to the finish?"

"If necessary."

The ground began to quake, gaining their attention as they flew out of the fortress and gazed around the outside. Theus could hear the sound of mumbling voice from the sky, even Taltus could hear the voice.

"Theus!" The voice echoed through the sky, rumbling even the clouds.

"Vindhler?!" Theus said.

"Theus, you must return home with haste! Destruction has come!"

"What do you mean?!"

"The foreign gods! They're combating above the land! Eragardia needs you to stop them!"

"Open the Asbru!"

Theus turned to Taltus as the Asbru opened above them. Blowing away the clouds like dust.

"It's two gods against one." Theus said. "Would be nice

if I could get some assistance."

Taltus grinned.

"After the battles we've been in together, you've helped my world. Now, I'll help your world."

Theus gave Taltus a nod as the Asbru fully opened and transported both Theus and Taltus from Earth to Eragardia.

CHAPTER THREE: WAR FORETELLS THE FUTURE

Beaming through the Asbru, Theus and Taltus arrived back in Eragardia to find the entire area seemly covered in dark clouds and lightning. Theus gazed ahead to the sound of thunder, seeing Zhor and Taraino clashing against each other with their weapons. Causing the rumble of the thunder. Below them were the people fleeing in fear from the collapsing buildings and lightning strikes.

"I take it those are the two gods you spoke of." Taltus said.

"Indeed. Aid me in stopping them from destroying my homeland."

Theus went and flew toward the thunder gods as Taltus followed. Inching closer to the foreign gods, a streak of dark lighting struck Taltus in the back, knocking him to the streets of Eragardia. Theus paused and looked down, seeing Taltus slowly standing up. Wondering what had happened, he noticed Taltus looking ahead to see the arrival of the dark elves, led by Voldor.

"Theus, deal with the gods. I'll take care of these invaders."

"Agreed."

Theus reached Taraino as he slammed his weapon across Zhor's back, causing him to collapse into the palace.

Taraino turned to see Theus and raised up his weapon.

"Why are you two fighting?" Theus asked.

"There can be only one god of thunder and it is I."

"You do not want to do this." Theus replied, as his hands began sparking lightning.

"I must. It is my purpose."

Taraino went for a strike against Theus, yet with his hands, he stopped Taraino's attack and grabbed his hammer, smashing it against Taraino, tossing him across the sky. Theus went and followed Taraino through the clouds of darkness as lightning fell around them to the ground. Meanwhile, Taltus bolted through the hordes of dark elves to reach Voldor. Taltus hovered in the air and let out his lightning vision, striking the dark elves in his sight. Voldor was impressed by the attack and even applauded.

"You have a gift." Voldor said. "Truly."

"I do not know who you are, but I suggest you return home before more things happen."

Voldor held up his spear and aimed it toward Taltus. Seeing it as a open to attack, Taltus flew with his fist in front, going for an attack against Voldor. Yet, Voldor dodged the punch by ducking underneath the arm of Taltus and swiping him with the spear into the ground. Voldor chuckled, raising the spear for the impalement. Seeing the blade, Taltus moved with speed to avoid the spear's coming attack. Turning around, Taltus snatched Voldor by his throat and drug him across the grounds of Eragardia before hitting him with a right punch, knocking him into one of the stables to the horses' displeasure.

"What are you?" Voldor arose with an explosion of elvish magic.

"I'm the titagod." Taltus answered. "The one and

only."

Still in the sky, Theus and Taraino fought with their weapons alongside the coming strikes of lightning. Theus went for a swipe with Mithrandir. Yet, Taraino deflected the blow before striking Theus in the chest with a palm strike. Theus stumbled in the air and while Taraino prepared for another strike, Zhor arose from behind him, moving through the dark clouds, smashing his hammer across Taraino's head. The blow knocked Taraino back onto the ground as he vanished from the air in their sights. Zhor gazed upward, seeing Theus.

"You cannot win this battle."

"I must. The two of you have brought nothing but tragedy to my home. After I offered you aid. You both claim there can be only one true god of thunder. Yet, I am a Millennium one."

Zhor let out a blood cry of a roar with his mallet in his hands, surging with lightning. Going in for a strike, Theus swiped him with Mithrandir, knocking Zhor back. stopping his movement in the air, Zhor stared toward Theus with only rage in his eyes. Seeking for another attack, he moved and was knocked from the sky by the returning Taraino. Theus flew toward them both and caused a great lightning storm which struck both thunder gods. Taraino and Zhor fell to the ground in front of the ongoing battle between Taltus and Voldor.

"These are the two gods?" Voldor questioned with disgust.

"They are." Theus said, hovering down from the sky. His eyes beaming with lightning. "Why are you here, Voldor?"

"You didn't think I would use this opportunity to take over your land? Poor Eragardian. Such ignorance like all the others."

Voldor let out a horn and blew, bringing forth more of his dark elf forces from the portal which opened around them. Theus saw the hordes coming through and there were dozens. Taltus stood up from the ground and flew into the sky to get a better look. Portals were opening across the streets of Eragardia.

"What's your plan?" Taltus asked Theus.

"You're outmatched, Millennium God of Thunder!" Voldor laughed.

"You know, I've always known your kind to be of traitors." Theus said. "Such is why I always had a contingency for your sudden arrival."

"Contingency?" Voldor questioned. "Of what nature?"

Theus raised his hand and struck he dark clouds with lightning. From them came forth rain, heavy rain. The rain poured upon them as Vindhler spoke to Theus from the distance. Stating they've arrived. Voldor stood boldly alongside his army. He wondered who Voldor spoke of and from the entrance of the city arrived the army of Wraith soldiers from Shadoheim and with them was their leader cloaked in piercing armored shadow from head to toe. The Wraith Knight. Voldor's dark eyes widen with anger and shock. He screamed as he saw Wraith Knight coming toward them. Both armies went for one another. Voldor rain past Theus and Taltus solely to reach the Wraith Knight.

"What of these two?" Taltus said, watching Zhor and Taraino return to their feet.

"I will deal with them. God to gods."

Theus stood ready as Taltus remained in case of backup. The three gods all prepared for another battle and the ground quaked. Catching them all by surprise as they each hovered above the ground. It cracked open, revealing Hadi. Theus clutched his fists to her arrival and Taltus stared. He remembered.

"I knew I felt the eerie presence of more than one thunder god."

"Why have you come here?!" Theus asked. "Do you wish for another battle?"

"No, Edenson. I came because this is off balance. The realms are shifting because of you three. Only one of you must remain."

"One of us?!" Zhor yelled. "Then it shall be I!"

"Not if I have anything to do about it." Taraino replied. "This day proves that I am indeed the true god of thunder. No matter the circumstance or cost."

Hadi stared at them. Sensing their power. She sighed.

"You two aren't from this realm nor this universe. You originate from a place I do not know."

"What are you saying?" Theus wondered.

"They're valuable. Very valuable. Therefore, I will take them."

The ground arose with dark spiked arms. Their hands snatched the legs of Zhor and Taraino from above and began to drag them into the glowing pit beneath them. The two gods struggled to get free from the hands as Theus, Taltus, and Hadi watched on. Zhor yelled with rage and smashed the arms with his hammer, causing them to let him loose as he rushed for Hadi. Quickly, she raised her right hand and froze Zhor in place before flicking him into the pit. Taraino continued to struggle after seeing Zhor fall into the ground. His eyes turned toward the three.

"This is not the end. I will find a way out and I will take my place as the definitive god of thunder. It is my destiny."

"No." Hadi replied. "It is not."

The arms collectively drug Taraino into the pit and it closed. Sealing shut as if it never opened.

"Where have you sent them?" Theus asked.

"They're being placed in my realm. In a chamber of silence. They will remain there under the end of days. When that time comes, they will be let loose, and they will fight again."

Hadi turned away as she vanished into a portal of her own making. Warning Theus their battle will come another day as she gave a sinister wink to Taltus.

"And is that all?" Taltus asked.

"For this day." Theus answered with a nod.

The two turned their attention toward the ongoing fight of the dark elves and the Shadoheimians. With the elves losing the fight and Voldor taking several strikes from the Wraith Knight, Voldor took the opportunity to escape as he saw Theus and Taltus arriving. Opening a portal, he rallied the remaining elves to make their exit and just as he entered the portal, Theus and Taltus landed on the ground in front of him. They didn't stop him from escaping.

"Next time you come here, it will be the end." Theus proclaimed.

"We shall see." Voldor answered, disappearing into the portal as it shut.

Wraith Knight approached Theus and they shook arms.

Theus introduced the Knight to Taltus and they greeted one another as warriors to the common cause. Wraith Knight's armor and design reminded Taltus of Swordman's look. Seeing it was more universal than he originally thought. Theus returned to the palace and saw the Trio and Lady Soya helping the others. Within the throne room Eden and Meredith spoke to each other concerning the foreign gods as Theus entered.

"You've returned." Eden said.

"I did and at the right time."

"Where are the two gods?" Meredith wondered. "Are they still here?"

"No. Hadi came and took them into her realm. She placed them in a trap until the end of days."

Eden nodded hearing the words.

"Very well. Such is good to hear."

Theus and Taltus aided the city with repairing and helping those who were caught in the crossfire of the battles. Seeing his time to return to Earth, Taltus left Eragardia. He greeted Theus before taking his leave. Meanwhile, as the guards continue to clean up Eragardia, they learned a portion of the prison had collapsed and Noldar had escaped.

GRAB THE COLLECTIONS

ABOUT THE AUTHOR

Ty'Ron W. C. Robinson II is the author of several works of fiction. Including the *Dark Titan Universe Saga*, *The Haunted City Saga*, *EverWar Universe*, *Symbolum Venatores*, *Frightened!*, *Instincts*, *Chevah Mythos*, *The Horde*, *Argoron*, *The Supreme Pursuer*, *Vanok*, *Dark Titan's The Dead Days*, and *Agent Trevor*.

Also of other books (*The Book of The Elect, etc.*) and One-Shot short stories.

More information pertaining to the author and stories can be found at darktitanentertainment.com.

Twitter: @TyRonRobinsonII
Vero: @tyronrobinsonii

Twitter: @DarkTitan_
Instagram: @darktitanentertainment
Facebook: @DarkTitanEnt

www.ingramcontent.com/pod-product-compliance
Lightning Source LLC
Chambersburg PA
CBHW030825200726
48288CB00004B/1396